Outskirts Press, Inc.
http://www.outskirtspress.com

Paperback ISBN: 978-1-9772-1184-2
Harback ISBN: 978-1-9772-2149-0

THIS BOOK BELONGS TO:

Once upon a time a very tall tree stood in a forest far away. Not only was it the tallest tree in the forest, but it was the most beautiful tree of all. This tree was also the happy home for many birds and small animals that lived in the forest.

First of all, a family of birds, including Papa Bird, Mama Bird and six little baby birdies lived in a nest way up on the top of the tree.

Every day Papa Bird flew all around the forest to find seeds and worms and bring them back to the nest so the little birdies would have food.

A busy family of squirrels also lived in the tall tree. The Mama Squirrel and the Papa Squirrel ran up and down the tree trunk and all around the branches carrying nuts and acorns back to their nest for the baby squirrels. They were busy all day, but they were very happy living in this tall, beautiful tree.

An entire family of fast-moving chipmunks also lived in the tall tree. They scurried up and down the tree and burrowed holes in the ground looking for nuts and seeds. Sometimes they ran so fast it seemed that no one could ever catch them.

A family of bunny rabbits lived in the bushes at the bottom of the tall tree. The Mama and Papa Rabbit hopped and ran all around the tree to find leaves, grass or wild berries to bring back to the little bunnies so they could munch and chew and grow to be big rabbits like their Mama and Papa.

All of these birds
and little animals
lived in harmony
in the tall tree and
were very happy. In
fact, they were one
big happy family.

One day two little mice, who were brothers, came to visit the tall tree. Their names were Sammy and Benny. They were looking for a new place to live and noticed that all of the birds and animals who lived in this tree were very happy.

Benny talked to Papa Bird and said, "My brother Sammy and I would like to live in this tree. Do you have room for two little mice?"

"Of course," said Papa Bird. "We also have parties every Friday night; you are welcome to join us. Just bring your own food."

So Sammy and Benny moved into the tall tree.

Everything was just fine for a few weeks, but Sammy— who was an adventurous little mouse—got very bored and decided to go out into the woods to investigate the area. When none of the other animals were looking, Sammy creeped under the bushes, squeezed through the high grass, and went on a long walk looking for some other mice to play with. He walked and walked for hours, and when he stopped to look around, he didn't recognize where he was.

He could no longer see the tall tree.

Sammy was lost.

Back at the tall tree, Benny was very sad. He had looked all day for his brother, but couldn't find him anywhere. He asked the squirrels, the chipmunks and the rabbits – but no one had seen Sammy.

Finally, he spoke to Papa Bird. "Have you seen my brother?"

"No," said Papa Bird, "but I will fly all around the forest to look for Sammy."

Papa Bird flew from the tall tree and looked down into the bushes and the high grass, and then near a big pond in the forest. He searched and searched, but he couldn't see Sammy anywhere.

So Papa Bird came back to the tall tree and talked to Benny who was very sad and missing his brother.

"Don't be sad, Benny. I know a special cat who lives far away in New York. His name is Mister Gray, and he is famous for being able to find lost animals. I'll send a message and ask him to come to our forest to find Sammy."

In just a few days, Mister Gray arrived at the tall tree. "Don't worry, Benny," he said. "I won't stop searching until I find your brother."

Mister Gray immediately began his search for Sammy by sniffing the ground and smelling the forest air trying to get the scent of a mouse as he walked away from the tall tree. He looked under all the bushes, he walked through the high grass; he checked the base of every tree. He walked and walked for miles. Finally he noticed something moving under a large leaf lying beneath a row of thick bushes. He stretched out his paw and lifted the leaf. And there he saw a little mouse, cuddled up on the ground, shivering in the cold.

Mister Gray had found Sammy.

Sammy was frightened at the sight of this large cat. But, Mister Gray smiled and said, "Don't be afraid, Sammy. Hop on my back, I'm going to take you home to the tall tree."

Sammy was so excited. He hopped onto Mister Gray's back and held on tightly as they raced through the forest. It was the most thrilling ride of his life!

When they arrived at the tall tree, all of the animals and birds came out to greet Sammy. "Welcome home!" they yelled.

Benny was so happy to see his brother. "Please don't ever run away again!" he said.

"Don't worry," said Sammy. "This is the best home ever. I'll never leave again."

That night Papa Bird organized a big party to celebrate Sammy's safe return. All the animals and birds sang and danced, and had a wonderful time.

Then they paused to cheer for Mister Gray—the special cat who rescued Sammy and brought him back home to his family of friends at the tall tree.

CPSIA information can be obtained
at www.ICGtesting.com
Printed in the USA
LVHW070537271119
638530LV00004B/195/P